SIMPLE CLUTTER

SIMPLE CLUTTER

Poems

by
James A. Zoller

RESOURCE *Publications* · Eugene, Oregon

Resource Publications
A division of Wipf and Stock Publishers
199 W 8th Ave, Suite 3
Eugene, OR 97401

Simple Clutter
By Zoller, James A.
Copyright©1998 by Zoller, James A.
ISBN 13: 978-1-5326-5922-5
Publication date 5/24/2018
Previously published by Mellen Poetry Press, 1998

for Donna

all the words
from first to last
and the silences as well

The following poems have been published in magazines, journals, and anthologies:

Untitled Domestic Poem*	*Blueline*
This, This**	*Blueline*
Rocking the House	*Blueline*
Sunday Morning	*The Christian Century*
News of Your Son	*Houghton College 1997 Christmas Card*
Webs and Windbreaks	*The Kentucky Poetry Review* reprinted in *Red Dancefloor*
At the Bus Stop	*Kudzu*
Widow	*Kudzu*
October 16	*Kudzu*
Soccer Match	*Literature: Reading Fiction, Poetry, Drama, and the Essay, 3/e*, Robert DiYanni, editor, McGraw-Hill
Equinox	*Other Poetry* (England)
Aging	*Other Poetry*
Provision	*Other Poetry*
Christmas List	*Other Poetry*
A Finger of Ground	*Oxford Magazine*
Watermelon Rind	*Oxford Magazine*
Sky Upon Us	*The Prose Poem: An International Journal*
Moment in Late Summer	*Red Dancefloor*
The Song	*Spree*
Old Man in Orchard with Scythe	*Zone 3*

*"Untitled Domestic Poem" appeared in the *Anthology of Magazine Verse & Yearbook of American Poetry* for 1984-85.

**"This, this" appeared in the *Anthology of Magazine Verse & Yearbook of American Poetry* for 1986-87.

There are so many stories,
more beautiful than answers.
-- *Mary Oliver*

I.

I.

It is possible that there is no other memory
than the memory of wounds.
-- *Czeslaw Milosz*

Once it seemed the function of poetry
was to redeem our lives.
But it was not. It was to become
indistinguishable from them.
-- *Brenda Hillman*

1954

A sign forbidding coloreds
sits in the window of a lighted restaurant
as we slow for Cheyenne
on the long drive from Golden Prairie.

Long before I am able to read,
that sign stands in memory
vivid as if I had seen it last night.

An Indian walks past. Like him we are a nation
of solitary figures, jackets turned
to the wind. It is October, already winter.

In time, a president will be shot dead,
thousands will die in a jungle war,
one brother will abandon his wife.

But that night as my parents exchanged words of pity
and sorrow, we are eating caramel popcorn,
noting the miracle of city lights after country dark --

the car warm, the hour late, eyes drowsy.
I look up in time to see the Indian,
lean, impassive, striding
past a sign I could not read, nor forget.

This, This . . .

Whenever it is dark in the house
I turn on a small light for comfort
a small light in the kitchen
over the sink.

In winter when day fades
I pull a chair to a window
to read by the light of sunset
news of a distant world,

and light from the kitchen
collects on the floor in dim puddles.
It reminds me that we are poor.
It reminds me of my mother

cutting sprouts from potatoes,
how she would call when I complained
"Come. Look!" water pouring from the tap
"Look, this we have in abundance."

The Song

hearing the whippoorwill
shriek its warning and lovesong
in the untended space between sunset and darkness
I am aware of my weaknesses
and the threat of frost

what is trivial
soberly governs my life
and what is consequential what is grave
comes to me through the air at dusk
calling my name like the birds

Rocking the House

a long grey shiv of rotting wood
lodges beneath the callous of the small toe joint
and screams when I walk, an abusive parrot
filling my foot with noise,
rocking the house.

I find a burned needle in the pin cushion
and burn it again;
it glows orange in the blue match flame,
the ritual fire.

what am I protecting myself against?
the spike of deadwood
I caught walking barefoot?
or the tempered steel,
the second, blackened, intruder?

I sit down to keep the room from moving,
I cross my legs yoga style,
the offended sole pulled upward,
my entire being strained toward its dark objective.

Wine, Red Roses, &
What Passes for Love

Early on the morning after Valentine's Day
a young man steals from my house
and drives away quietly into the darkness
in a car he'd parked down the street.

He drives without headlights back past my yard.
Though the steps spoke and a rush of cold air found me,
he made less noise descending the stairs
and closing my front door than the mice

who slip in when days get short and nights cold
through cracks no wider than a nail paring.
I hear them at hours when mere men are sleeping.
Then I set traps and patch holes until

the nights are quiet again and I can hear the moon
raising itself longingly into the trees.

After the lurid red of brakelights at the corner
the street is dark and my house is still.
His coed, my renter, has returned to bed.
Surely they had not thought to find

my light spilled under the kitchen door, or me
sitting at my table. Already I had boiled coffee,
stoked the furnace, listened to heat rise
up to the room where my trespasser slept contentedly.

I write down what I saw to be sure of it
and to hedge the corrosion of memory. Let us not
be deceived nor forgetful. In lieu of commitment
she got what he might carry:
wine, red roses, and what passes for love.

Moment in Late Summer

the children rush in
tattered with bits of straw
brown from the loft
with its ropeswing
its hay mountains
& its mice.

breathless
& loud from play
they
demand water
& eyes
for the tales
they have
just
discovered.

suddenly they
vanish, the silence
filling
with flies
from the open door.

Missing You in Toledo

Outside Toledo where the train has stopped
          to wait for tracks ahead to clear
I record simple observations:
          a red-yellow-green totem
-- Eagle, snake, bear --
          faces the tracks,
A refugee in some back yard,
          scanning travelers, anonymous, lost.

From daybreak I note the earth has flattened:
          broad farmland, featureless,
So incredibly black. Between field and tracks
          through a gully, telephone poles,
Globe-wrapping miles of wire
          and voices voices voices
But not yours, not mine.

In back lots abutting the tracks junked stoves,
          refrigerators without doors,
Washing machines orange with rust,
          miles of these stark objects --
The guts of kitchens sluiced into ditches, discarded.

Now the train begins to move,
　　　the bright puzzling totem slips past.
It is, I know suddenly, an icon,
　　　fiercely shaped to keep hope alive.

But what, as it reappears on this page, can I tell you
　　　that might reduce the miles,
The growing gap between us?

I have missed you in Toledo.

Untitled Domestic Poem

in the kitchen
with the drafty floor
the temperature dipped
and I turned the heat on
for the first time since early May

radiators bang
an old tune I'd forgotten

we fought it
vowed to live in sweaters
long wool underwear

and how we fought it
but this morning
answering the clock in the cold
in the black silk of October
I gave in

moved by the dim light
of your blue hands

Winding the Clock

It had belonged to the second of grandmother's husbands,
my step-grandfather, now thirty years dead,
an orphan who emigrated at ten, surrendering
his British childhood. He became as american
as anyone, cheering when my father
went off to the second war.
He was, when I knew him, a traveling salesman
for American Beauty Macaroni.
He smoked Winston cigarettes.

His clock is nearly all we have of him now:
its straight black hands held by wire,
cherry cabinet grown dark and somber
with years, brass pendulum tarnished.

Centered on the dining room wall,
it keeps an average time.
On the floor across the room,
another useful artifact:
a heavy trunk with "FWJackson"
stenciled on the end. Broken leather handles.

For years the clock sat in my father's basement
frustrating his attempts to keep it running.
But I have mastered the works.
As with so much of life, small jolts,
vibrations in the wall skew its balance
and the pendulum stops. I set it right.

And sometimes, when it refuses realignment,
I let it rest. A week it takes. Two.
I push the pendulum now and then,
adjust its up-rightness. It always resumes
when it is ready. And I, for one, respect that.

Red Mitten

> One day at noon as you walk out to the mailbox
> He'll snatch you up --
> a woman beside the road like a red mitten.
> > --Anne Sexton

God come down one day at noon
as you
reach into your mailbox for the electric bill
and the Instant Millionaire Sweepstakes flier.
He plucks your soul
just as sudden just as clean
as one might find her
purse snatched on a subway platform
in the confusion of trains.

As you draw your hand out, quickly,
as you recognize the price of kilowatts, as you
spot the redwhite&blue Winner's envelope
with its promise of heaven NOW,
your lights go out, your plug
pulled before the adrenaline of joy
that might have saved you kicks in,
and your soul skitters away on the breeze,
a dry leaf.

Odd that you Didn't Quite Believe Anyway
--you who pondered the Who of God, the What, the Why
--you who hated Big Daddy --
Who else would make all those otherworldly promises
straightfaced?
The Instant Millionaire Sweepstakes flier has your name
and a picture of St. Thomas (Paradise, for the rich,
as you would have been),
but God has already sucked-up your soul and moved on

13

your body discarded, forgotten by the road
as you
fall slowly, dramatically, a letter, an envelope,
a red mitten, bone and hair, housedress & apron,
hands still damp, for school girls
to find, to say "What is it?" "Who is it?"
Knowing nothing about you or God
or the cost of keeping things alive

or the dark cancellation of your smile.

October 16

the late wind and night air
arrives bearing frost
shaking its white seeds

the corn in the field
is black and rustling
like pebbles in brown sacks

soon it will be winter
the voice of a woman with child
calls out in the black air

I rise in the solid predawn
make coffee and sit
in a circle of light at the kitchen table

trying again to read a future
in the mug
or the wood's holy grain

Stars

little one
the stars who sleep late
in the morning sky
are even now being shaken.

please, let me
help you sit up.
I will hold your hand
on the stairs.

little one
the sky is red;
over the hill outside the window
mother sun has her fires going.

It will be warm soon.
her many children, look, look,
are leaving their beds
each with his bowl & catechism.

Summons

Long before the sun warms the far hill
my son in his dark room talks nonsense,
rattling the bars of his crib,
idly clanking the Busybox gizmos with his foot.

In the kitchen, I wait,
fire prompted and nursed to warm our rooms;
coffee held, consulted like a friend.
After prayers, my daily foray with words.

I delay going to fetch him:
awake, but not in pain or danger.
Then, a scarlet slash across the darkness,
where earth meets heaven.

I set aside my pencils, my simple clutter,
my carved moment. I rise to take up my child.

Watermelon Rind

Cloves are what I remember
in the watermelon pickles,
floating among the green cubes,
tiny clubs with spiked heads.

Long after he died we ate,
opening the last jars
for Sunday dinner, the way
it used to be -- as if

he were still there,
perhaps gone to the kitchen
momentarily. Momentarily.
Oh, we ate the pickles all right,

commenting on them
as if nothing had changed --
the last batch with too much
of something, perhaps cloves,

and while we ate we talked
occasionally of him, the way
one eats pickles here and there,
the way one fills

natural pauses. We finished
the pickles without knowing
it, thinking more were
in the cellar,

surprised, briefly,
that all the jars had been emptied,
cleaned and returned
to the pantry

where they sit awaiting
the next curator of pickles,
though no one has had the ambition.
We throw out the rind now:

it has become summer garbage.
And we talk less of my father,
even on Sundays at dinner.
It seems natural that way.

Widow

fog lies in gullies,
along the roadways.

in the marsh where beech are rooted in water
the leaves turn early.

the moon is distant and wan,
a quarter past new.

later, when the moon lies on the horizon
like a pale pumpkin

and trees on the hillsides
are naked

and screens on the summer homes
are shuttered

and ponds are glazed,
you will return to the roadways alone.

how like death is the fog
that waits in the gully

how like friends
the stark black trees.

Aging

take the earthen bowl from its shelf
set it on the brown table

let us hide a morsel in it
to discover at another time

when the future
demands its last meal

A Finger of Ground

As boys in my father's car,
we passed through Kentucky heading east
-- or west, I don't recall.
As the words "bluegrass" and "thoroughbred"
materialized, somehow, we wondered
at every grazing horse and every fenced field,
though I was small and memory wanders.

What I do recall, distinctly, is West Virginia
and that it was raining, hard. We followed
a road that followed a river, swollen
over its banks, swirling around tree trunks,
a terrified cat on a careening plank,
water muddy, rancid with debris. I knew
in seconds it would swallow the road.

At one point my father, calm as ever, drove
out on a peninsula of asphalt
onto an old narrow low-bellied bridge heading
for another line of black road
in the eternal distance, slowing
on the humming steel deck, eyes fixed.
If Hell is flat-out terror,

this was Hell. I looked up
from the waters that churned and tugged
at the floorboards to the steel beams
that seemed neither sturdy nor graceful,
that resembled nothing so much
as a child's frail erector set
arching dimly into the smokey low clouds.

22

Though I have neglected whatever vows I made,
I remember the cat's terror
and the swift water of West Virginia.

And when we reached that far finger of ground
and we all, mother and boys, breathed again, together,
my father reset his cap and smiled and drove on.

II.

--And all of a sudden
In the midst of that silence
It seems possible
To live simply
On the earth.
  --Charles Simic

Sunday Morning

I have learned from forty years
the fine art of sitting pews --
head up, mouth still, eyes focused,
following ideas through swamps of logic,
through thickets of analogy, high prose.

After training the others, your siblings,
in this fine art I help you climb my lap
seeking diversion. How so? This preacher
is not so bad as preachers go,
reasoned, careful, restrained.

Together we trace the picture on the program,
we fill in o's and a's and e's inside until
the page is full of clean holes
like signs along rural roads in our county.
This, and still I am able to listen.

Later, taking a blank paper intended for notes
you begin looking about, touching it occasionally
with my black pen. "I make dots when I see something,"
you whisper, loudly, holding up a picture of chaos.
Patiently, you connect. "It's a world now,"

you laugh. There it is in a nutshell.
I put my finger to your lips to remind you,
though it's not so bad: a pure response, a simple act.
We should do so well, waiting on the preacher
to make a world, now.

I Gaze Intently

The face I face is my
        face writ backward.
The hand I lift I lift
        opposing my hand.

What I must see clearly as eye
        raises hand with razor
Is the absolute literalness
        of the image.

Old Man in Orchard with Scythe

far down through the orchard
      among rows of gnarled trees
            he removes his shirt and begins again

the breeze heavy with cut grass
      and turned soil
            he sighs and swings the scythe

behind him the grass lies in bundles
      it is green and new and cuts easily
            later (drier) it will resist

he mows smoothly from tree to tree
      noting woodchuck trails
            cutting low for mouse or shrew

now and again he stops to light a cigarette
      to check the small hard apples
            he pulls a whetstone from his pocket

he slips the oval stone along the thin blade
      finding the bright metal on the edge
            with its taste for blood

Webs & Windbreaks

across the valley
fields laid out in irregular rectangles
bordered by windbreaks & woodlots
by land long since out of cultivation

early in the morning
clouds hide the clumps of buildings
and distant blue silos
clouds roll against this very window

it is September
& I wait for the sun
to melt this fog back into the ground
soon the leaves will change

and the woods
will be deadly with hunters
and the corners
of this old house

will fill with webs
fragile clouds of silk
that know the value of stealth
and little surprises

Equinox

we always come back to the white pumpkin
        to the wicker basket of half-ripe
                rotting peaches,
        to bruised tomatoes
                on a cookie sheet by the window.

brown leaves blow against the foundation
        on the north side.

white smoke rises in the early air
        as the old man kindles his flannel
                and his bones,
        as the children wave and holler,
        as cars hurry through the streets,
        as a black spider waits on lace nets
                among blackberry canes.

I rise to find darkness
        and ice in the cups.

and the clock spinning its slow wheel,
        sensing harvest.

Soccer Match
> How graceful the small before danger.
>
> Theodore Roethke

From a hillside
where fathers and mothers
gather with lawn chairs
some boys, small in their red uniforms,
converge on other boys in their blue,
then scatter,
rush in waves like infantry,
then clot,
drawn across their tidy battlefield
to a tiny white ball
that eludes them.

Suddenly the ball shoots
from the surge of red and blue
beneath the diving keeper
into the goal net.

Red fists and shouts rise,
voices smoothed to a roar by wind.
Boys in red converge, retreat
toward their own end.
Boys in blue stand, sullen
even from this distance,
the clear posture of defeat.

A serious event, I am aware,
though not tragic. Once
it would have ruined my bus-ride home.
A late arriver I have witnessed a crucial moment.

The boys grow larger as I walk downhill.
I spot my son
expressionless but for the hard set of jaw
returning to mid-field
to begin again. That's it, I say.
I feel palpable disappointment, anger in the air,
an elusive renewal of determination.

These blue and red figures
become men as I draw near,
covered with dirt and sweat. I can distinguish
between the ragged shouts, I see faces
bright with blood.

Run hard, I find myself shouting against the wind.
Keep to your lane, I rage from the sideline.
I feel myself somehow passing the ball, son,
as you close on the goal.

Where October Leads

Have you forgotten how
                October
        shifts
quickly
        from gold/
        yellow
through rainbows of red
                into
browns and brown/
        yellow?

In this morning's cold
        rain
branches grow
                prominent
        like veins on an old man's arm --

a skinny old man
        whose body has shed
its vibrant summer colors
        who stands transfixed
                over smoldering fires,
                        over smokey
                pungent fires.

Migrant

already the leaves
are departing
and the trees remember

the sky
is like the ocean at St. Croix
--but how cold!

even now
as geese fly south
with blue feet
someone deep in these roots
is closing valves

and the flowers
those little souls

at the end of the season the doors
clang eternally in their ears

What I See When I Get There

As I go
sunlight slides beneath my feet
        irradiates my plumed breath,
                sets the aspen aflame.
Stars, perhaps fallen, spark in the grass.
The road is bright,
the road is long and black from where I stand.

Around me
reds of sugarmaple, flushred, newly wounded,
reds of sumac, stainred, bold, deep
rustred of ivy
red of oak, brickred, hard brownred
        sunburnished
bluegreen bruise red of barberry
        crimson berried
                festive crabapplered.

Even at high noon
red of leaves I have no name for
        ragged edged scarlet edged
                smoothedged heart red.

This year, red-tinged mountain ash
        red-orange, berried
redbush
deep brilliant redmaple red, kimono red
        birthmark red

red of sunset
        oozing along the horizon
                blazing behind skeletal hardwood
                        sparking stars on eastward plum hills,
                draining, then, quickly
        red purple to blues
varied blues buried reds, grown deeper,
grown impossibly deep
grown beyond imagining

beyond black slowly circling the earth
beyond the window
        that looks in on me.

Sky Upon Us

We don't think like this when the sky is upon us, snow thick in the air from clouds almost within reach. Then, we think of the falling snow riding the wind over and through the trees, blinding us, or snow drifting from the sky in deep deep quiet as if snowfall had meaning if only we could stop, if only we could hear those minutely crashing forms.

But this morning the snow is on the ground and the sky grows deeper blue by the minute and the sun, dropping black shadows from tree and hill, strikes brilliantly across the snowscape.

We blink and haul our tube to the top of the hill, blink at the bright sun on the single packed trail to the bottom, sit one atop the other on the tube, slide quickly in the hard groove.

Together we sail over the ice, over bumps and pits; gain speed as any falling object; learn gravity, minutely aware of distance time inertia, mouths open with astonishment, voices torn out and lost to the wind; sail through the run; sail into deep snow beyond, plowing, gliding, spraying cold powder about until the tube stops and we fly apart, tumble, collide.

How different this all is: this cold horizontal world, the bite of the cold snow on our faces, the sky like deep immaculate water, the shocks our bodies absorb and mine remembers. I roll myself over, struggle against the soft snow to gain my feet; the sky blazes, the snow dazzles, you scamper toward the steep path just as laughter and shouts collide in my ears and lungs, catching up.

Shooting Accident

on my knees in the shallow snow
I strain to topple
the instant the bullet burst
and the belly tears to let it enter
I think how long I have had
to live in pain

blood runs in one thick black river
toward the earth's center
toward some strange man
it knew before me

already, I think as I lie down beside it
how terribly deep the snow is

Provision

February thaw and rain
have turned the road to mire
slowing travel

a week ago
before temperatures rose
and set the streams free
we plowed the snow
and hauled our pigs to the slaughterhouse

where they are hanging now
over a fire that does not touch them

Safety First
  (Belfast, NY)

Just past the full lot at Harley's Pub
& bare-chested Hammer's safe-T billboard

19A cants left, then
        dog-legs right

sharp enough to slow one's car
        for Main Street

& drive truckers down to low range.

Slowly, now -- straighten the wheel,
          gather speed --

a worn blue house-turned-bar, its
lot full, gas & convenience store

Bar-B-Q out on the common
quietly full of snow.

Opposite these
a trailer, one rusty white house,

side street, car-filled lot, cinderblock bar
lit by red Coors and blue Labatts

neon on-the-fritz.

Dimly lit store facades flash by
           pink and blue.

Without so much as a thought,
one eyes mud-speckled pickups,

       grime-dulled stationwagons,
           like cows nosing the curb

       where a small abandoned dog
           or some wild boy waits

       to dash beneath headlamps,
           a flash at the corner of the eye.

For an instant
for one hard thump of your heart

       you know that boy, he is yours
       vulnerable, dangerous

           but, no
           yours is . . .

Then,
the hill crests,

    drops

and one is
        cruising
                again,

one is drawing a long, slow breath, again,

having slowed
for Belfast,

having left it
            all
                    behind.

Faith
    for Charles Simic

something within the edge of the woods
    at the precise point of obscurity

something I have been moving toward all along

something with a voice, not raised, not strident,
    not above all articulated but there, distinct
    as a mushroom being sliced

something to embrace the paradox of parallels
    fusing where land meets sky

something rooting in mud-hovels,
    breaking like light at Chartre

something without shape, substance, body, form, organs
    which I dissect with infinite care

something I have laid my hands on, have spoken to,
    have forgotten in the labyrinth of waking

something within the dried fruit of infinity like a seed

something beneath the war statuary,
    beneath boots of faceless infantry,
    beneath banners of a new order
    that bleeds in the public square like an old woman
    dying perpetually, despised and heroic

something bound in the webs of cosmology
    beneath a dazzling, vacant sky

something about which has always
       irrevocably been said, ah! yes . . .

something that even now
       sits on a small folding chair tipped to the wall
       just past the circle of light
       and laughs at this nonsense.

Salman Rushdie

who, by his own confession,
        is not a religious man,
for the sake of the myth, the lively sentence
strikes at the feet of Islam
with words like stones.

Unlike any response
one might have imagined, another

who, though learned,
        is not a man of letters,
for the sake of the myth, the life sentence,
strikes at free, or careless, speech
with words in stone

that one can neither dodge
nor revise.

There is a time for planting
        and a time for harvest;
                for war and for peace;
a time for the full moon
        and a time for eclipse.

Now the serious pondering of fate:
      the religious man
who has died and gone before his Maker
      and the secular man
who, precluding God with his almighty IF,
      seeks reconciliation
of his views with the Other's --

whose words still linger
      in the air
somewhere overhead.

Confession

In my prayers
the dying are born away
on wagons with stone wheels

flowers bloom without end
In my prayers
leaves fall

clouds sweep overhead
followed by birds
who are cared for

In my prayers
I tremble
God overwhelms me

In my prayers
I hear stone wheels
approaching

Chiaroscuro

The hand that holds the pencil holds
      a sword of words, holds
      the world, is the hand
that says "follow me" along this
      black on white path, through this
      moon struck landscape, changes
world-at-large to earth-under-foot.

What eye sees I see, head holds:
      shoes with leather soles scuff
      stone and leaf strewn path
dappled in full moonlight, all birds
      silent now, even wide-eyed
      silent-winged owl who leaves
just traces of struggle writ wisely in blood.

News of Your Son

A tiny star
in the black wilderness
of a winter morning,
the air like iron.

Wind has ceased,
boots crunch in the snow.

The horses, still shadows;
houses on streets below
the pasture
closed down, like sleeping faces.
Slow smoke of banked fires.

Now you on this errand
at this hour
in this deadly air
in the pit of winter,
looking for someone
to share your joy at this news . . .

At the Bus Stop

the car stops
it is time to get out
the snow
luminous
sparkling near the street lamps

the road is plowed
but I am alone on it
as if it had been cleared
a hundred dark years ago
and everyone is dead now

or weary of travel

Christmas List

A knife for salvation
A book for its doors

A voice or a fence for freedom
            either will do
Mice for comfort

A clock for anxiety
A pen, a pen to live by

Hands to shape the air
Window casings to sing in the freshening wind

A moment, a chair
& light

Yes, a little circle of light

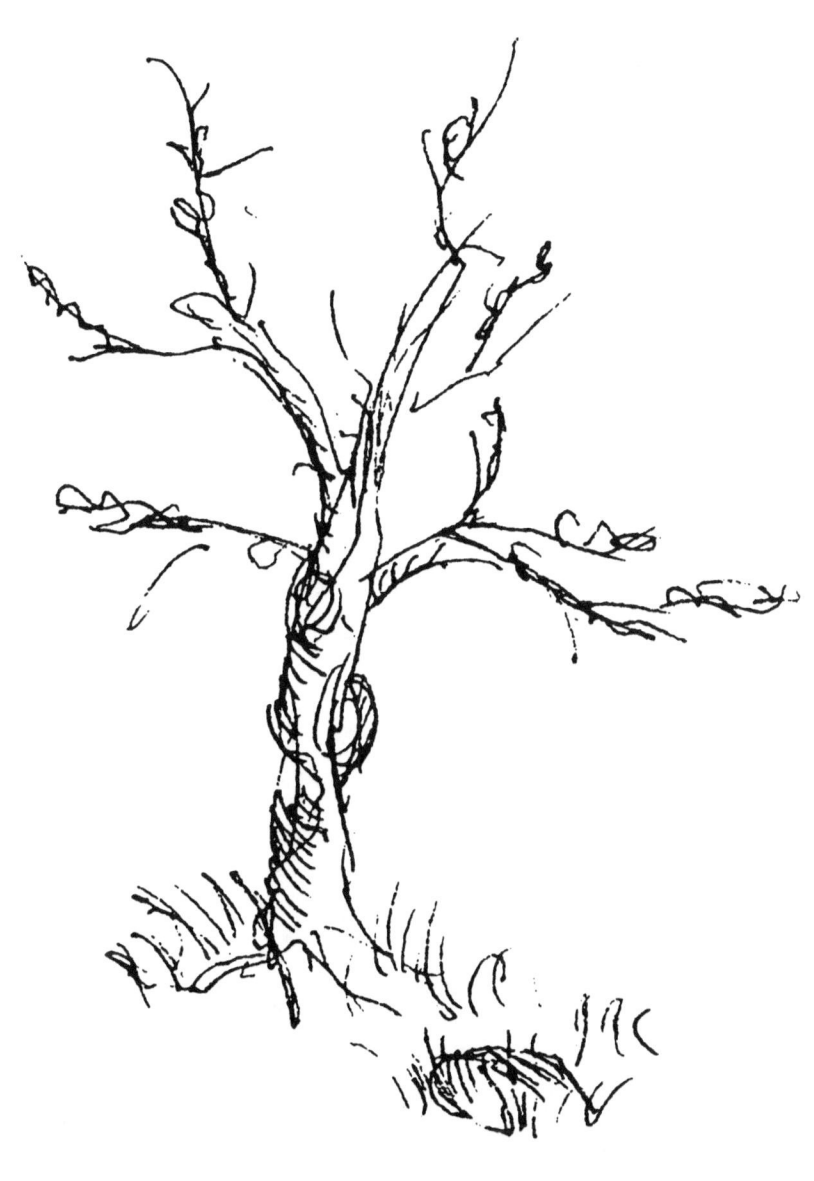

www.ingramcontent.com/pod-product-compliance
Lightning Source LLC
Chambersburg PA
CBHW071316200626
46813CB00015B/2232